FIVE HIDING OSTRICHES

Barbara Barbieri McGrath   Illustrated by Riley Samels

Charlesbridge

Five little ostriches,
huddled in one spot.

The first one said,

"It's getting rather hot."

The second one said,

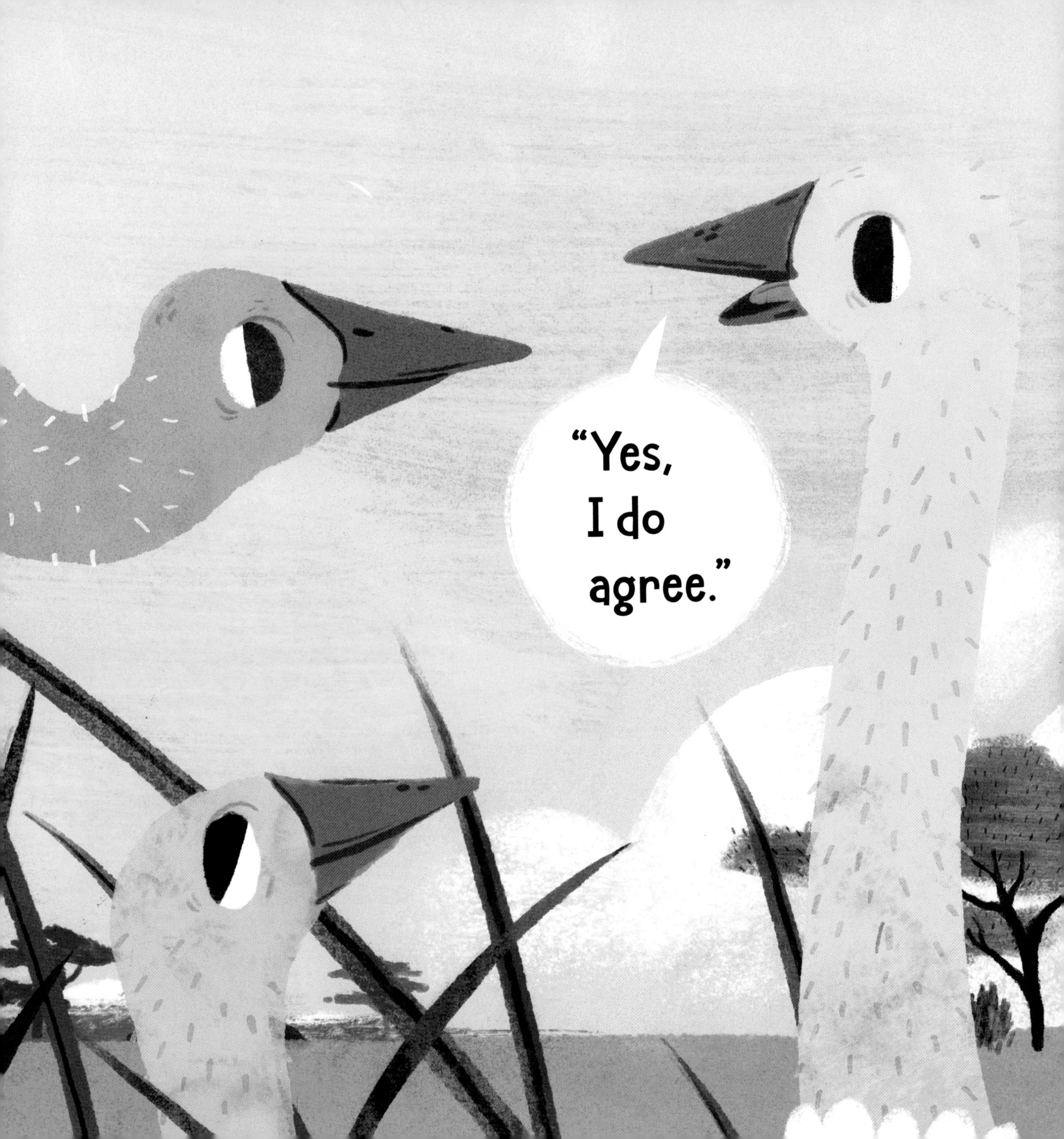
"Yes, I do agree."

The third one said,

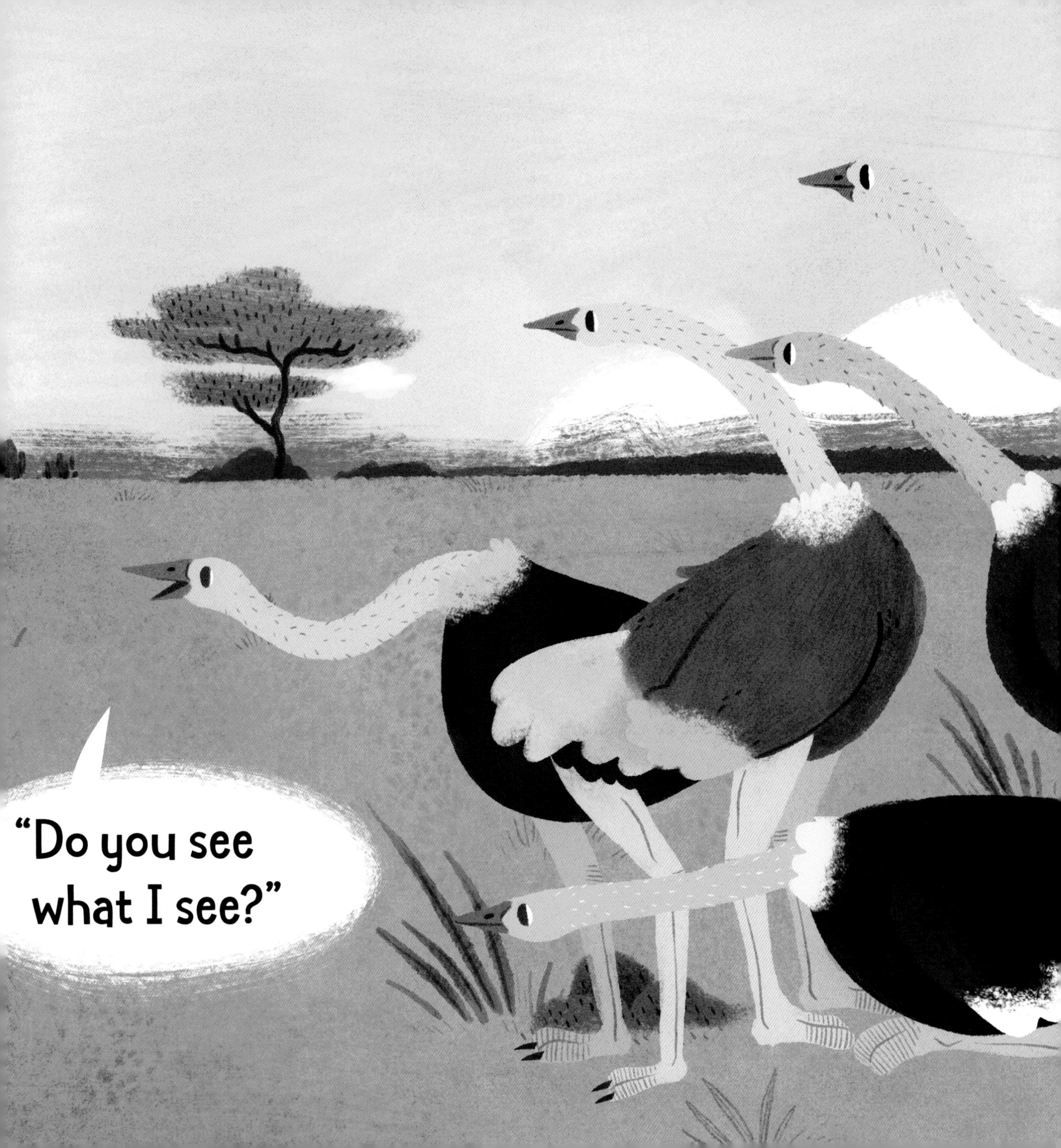
"Do you see what I see?"

The fourth one said,

"Let's run and run and run!"

The fifth one said,

"This might be kind of fun!"

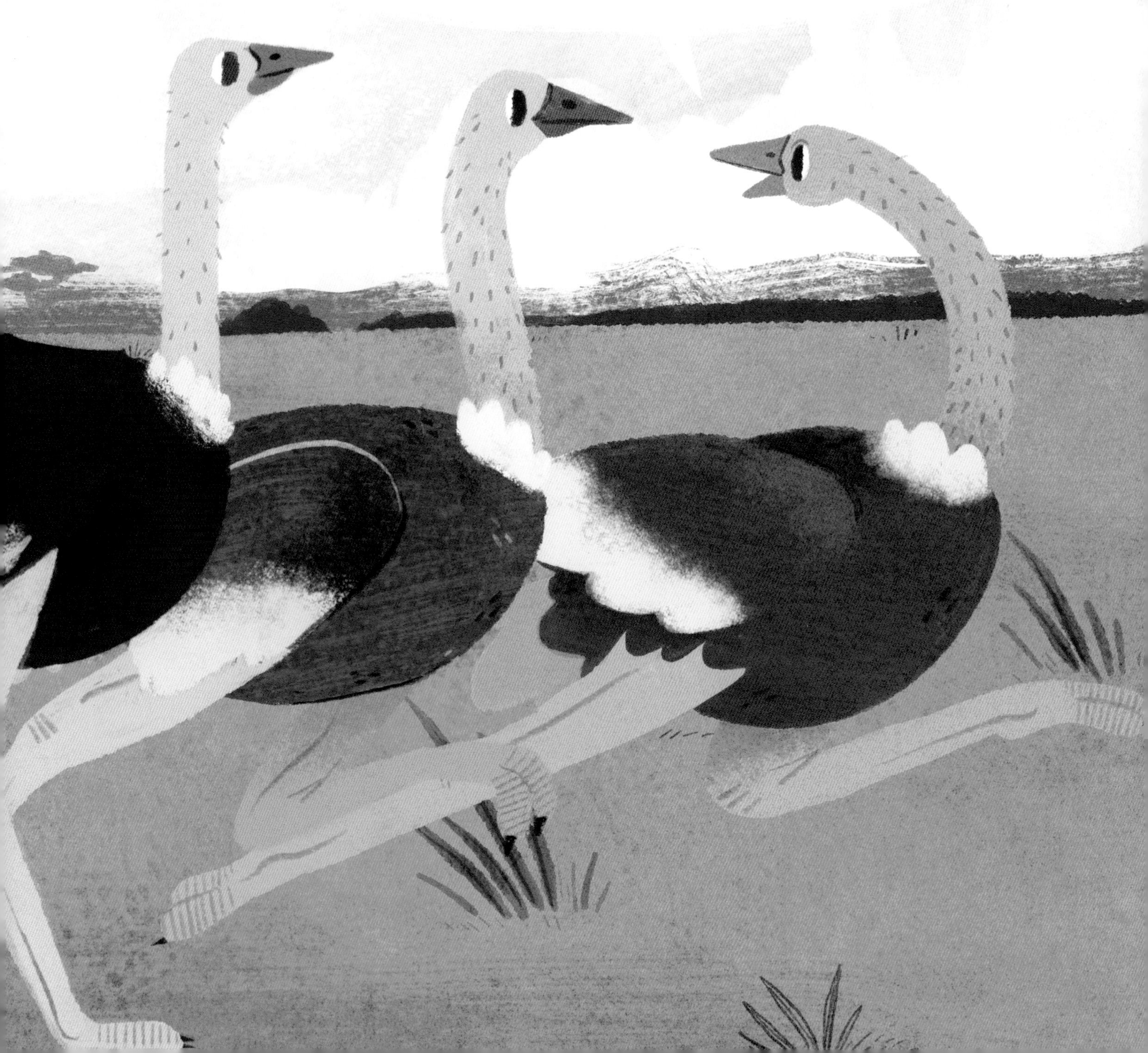

Stomp! Stomp!

went ostrich feet as they hurried through the brush.

Then five fast birds
stopped to whisper,

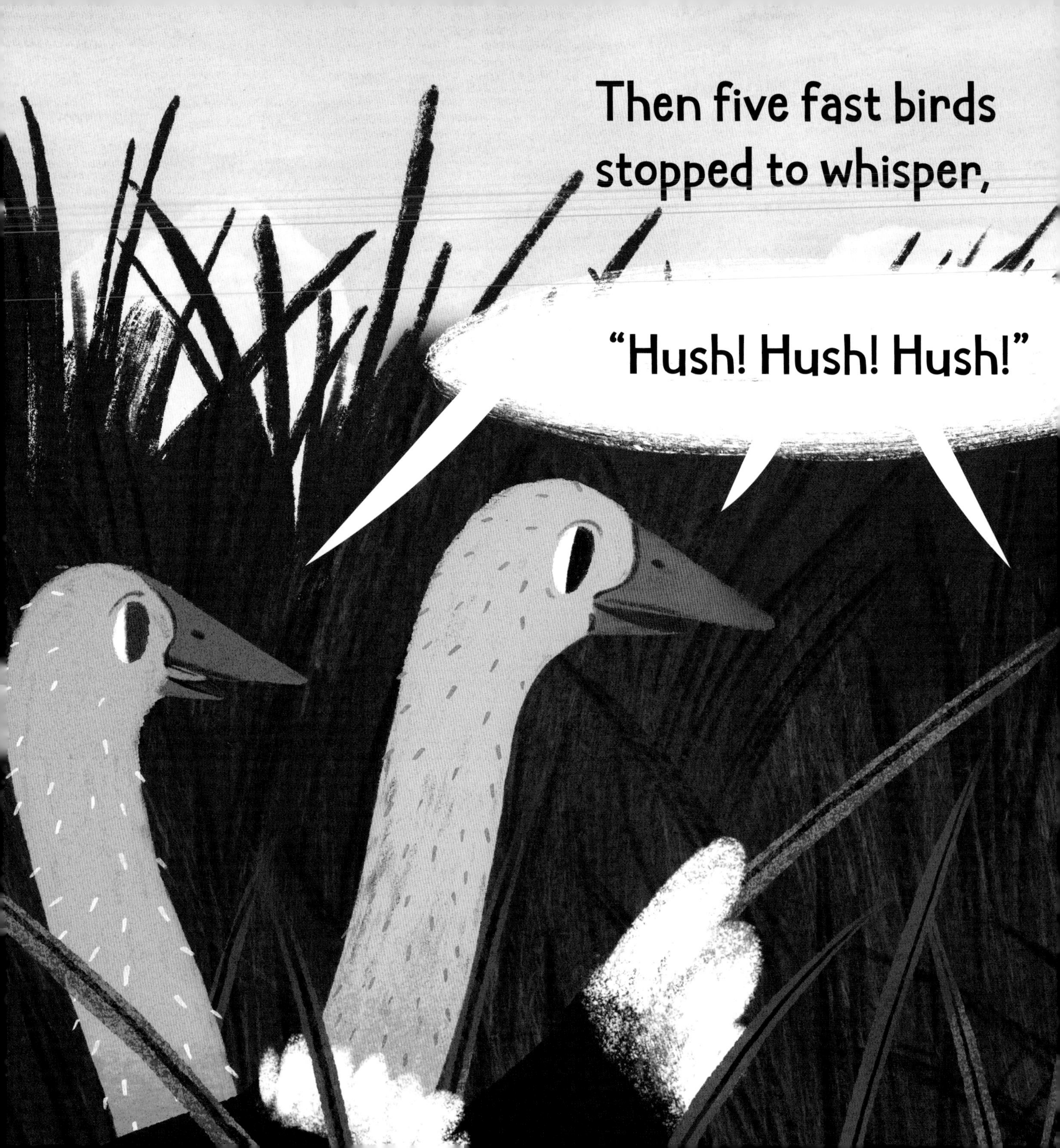

Five hiding ostriches
heard the lion getting near.

The first one said . . .

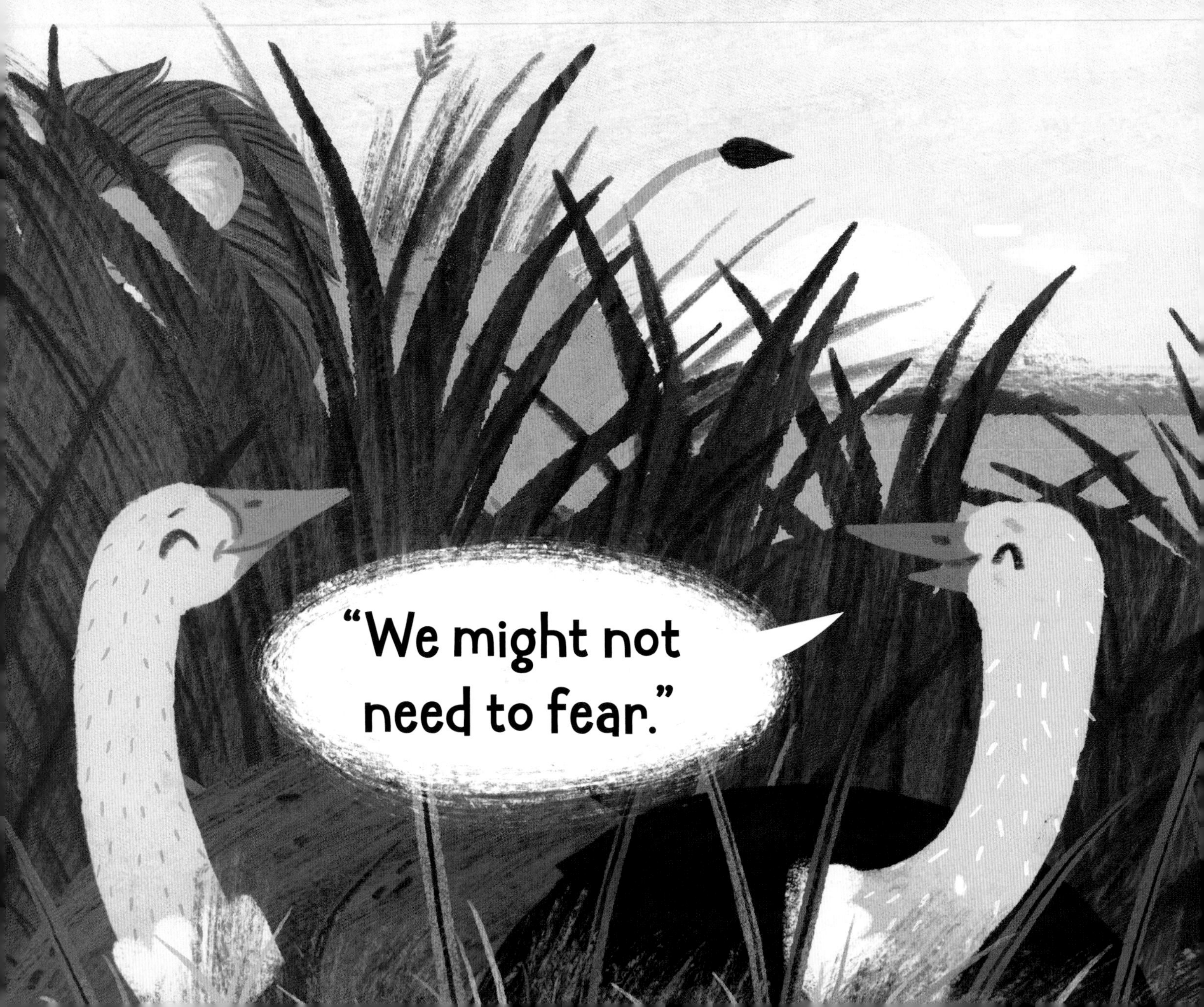

The second one said,

"Let's dash to the hill."

The third one said,

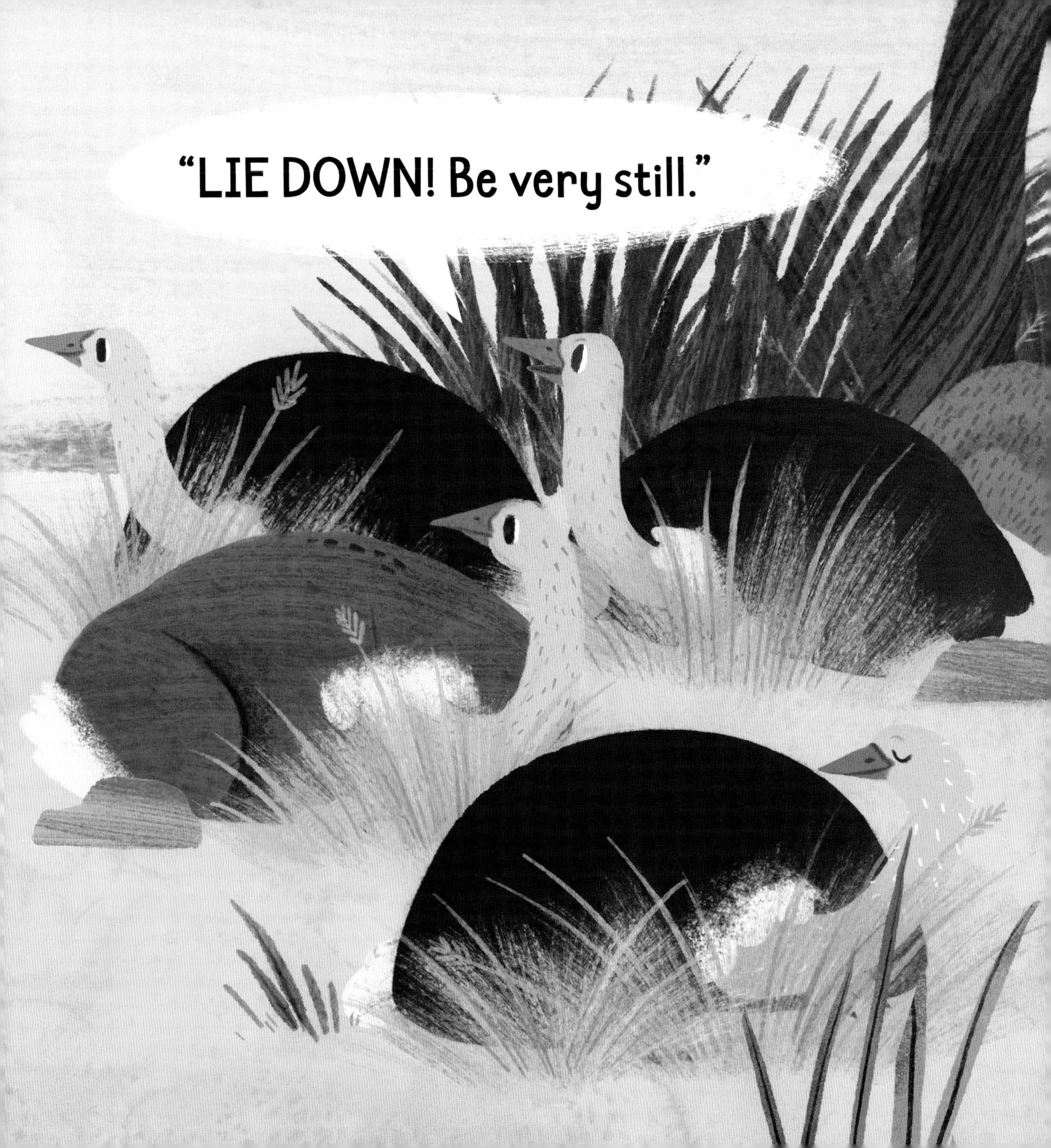
"LIE DOWN! Be very still."

The fourth one said,

"Pretend you are a rock."

The fifth one said,

"And none of us
should talk."

ROAR boomed the big lion, coming closer for a peek.

Stumped, the lion finally said,

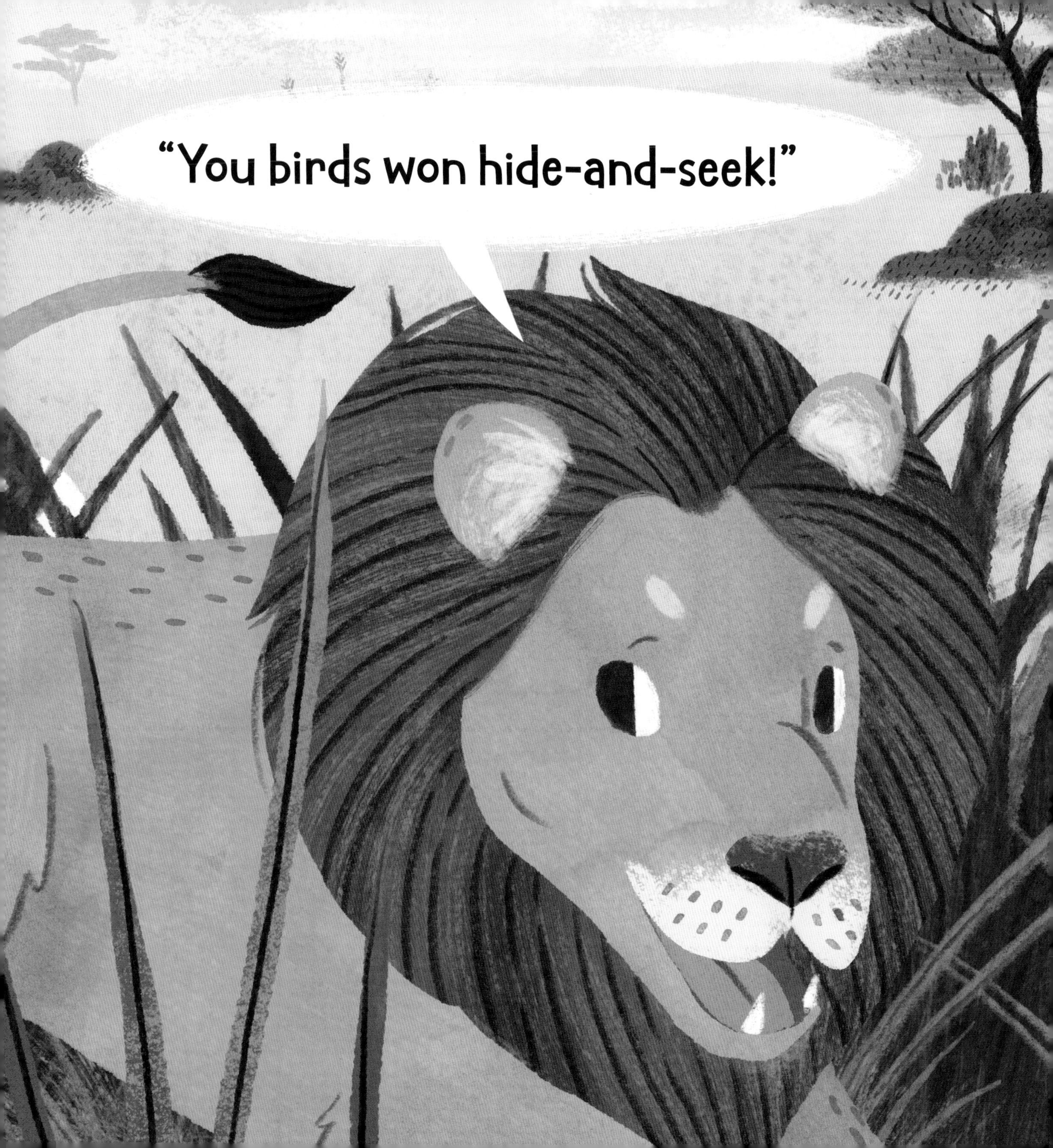
"You birds won hide-and-seek!"

A ROCK 'N' ROAR Game

It was once thought that ostriches bury their heads in the sand to hide from danger (like lions!). But this is not true. Instead, they lie down, stretch their necks out, and put their heads down on the ground to disguise themselves as rocks—an unusual but clever way of playing hide-and-seek. Ostrich necks and heads camouflage with the ground, and their bodies look like big boulders.

In the spirit of ostrich (and lion) behavior, here's a ROCK 'N' ROAR game to play!

1. Gather a group of three or more friends. Have one friend or an adult be the Game Leader. Split the rest of the group into either Ostriches or Lions.

2. When the Game Leader yells, **"HIDE-AND-SLEEP!"** Lions, lie down, close your eyes, and pretend to sleep. Ostriches, stand up, flap your wings, and find a place to hide.

3. When the Game Leader yells, **"ROCK 'N' ROAR!"** Ostriches, crouch down in your hiding spot and pretend to be a rock. Lions, slow-crawl on your hands and knees and roar as you prowl around looking for hiding Ostriches.

4. When the Lions have found all the Ostriches, mingle in a circle. Ostriches flap your wings, and Lions roar!

With love to Willa James—B. B. M.

To my parents, who fostered my love of both the arts and animals—R. S.

Text copyright © 2022 by Barbara Barbieri McGrath
Illustrations copyright © 2022 by Riley Samels
All rights reserved, including the right of reproduction in whole or in part in any form. Charlesbridge and colophon are registered trademarks of Charlesbridge Publishing, Inc.

At the time of publication, all URLs printed in this book were accurate and active. Charlesbridge, the author, and the illustrator are not responsible for the content or accessibility of any website.

Published by Charlesbridge
9 Galen Street
Watertown, MA 02472
(617) 926-0329
www.charlesbridge.com

Printed in China
(hc) 10 9 8 7 6 5 4 3 2 1

Illustrations done digitally
Display type hand-lettered by Riley Samels
Text type set in Digby by Amy Dietrich
Printed by 1010 Printing International Limited in Huizhou, Guangdong, China
Production supervision by Jennifer Most Delaney
Designed by Jon Simeon and Kristen Nobles

Library of Congress Cataloging-in-Publication Data
Names: McGrath, Barbara Barbieri, 1954– author. | Samels, Riley, illustrator.
Title: Five hiding ostriches/Barbara Barbieri McGrath; illustrated by Riley Samels.
Description: Watertown, MA: Charlesbridge, [2022] | Audience: Ages 3–7. | Audience: Grades K–1. | Summary: Told in rhyming text, five little ostriches hide from a lion, run through the bush, and find themselves in an innocent game of hide-and-seek.
Identifiers: LCCN 2020051641 (print) | LCCN 2020051642 (ebook) | ISBN 9781623541965 (hardcover) | ISBN 9781632899811 (ebook)
Subjects: LCSH: Ostriches—Juvenile fiction. | Lion—Juvenile fiction. | Hide-and-seek—Juvenile fiction. | Stories in rhyme. | Picture books for children. | CYAC: Stories in rhyme. | Ostriches—Fiction. | Lion—Fiction. | Hide-and-seek—Fiction. | Counting. | LCGFT: Stories in rhyme. | Picture books.
Classification: LCC PZ8.3.M1592 Fk 2022 (print) | LCC PZ8.3.M1592 (ebook) | DDC [E]—dc23
LC record available at https://lccn.loc.gov/2020051641
LC ebook record available at https://lccn.loc.gov/2020051642